Darren Richards is a creative communicator and author. His passion is releasing others to use their gifts to serve the fatherless and oppressed. He has been writing professionally for over a decade for Youth for Christ, as well as ghost-writing for CEOs and writing talks, sermons and scripts for short films. He has extensive experience of working strategically in the voluntary sector, managing national prison projects and arts programmes, championing diversity, and mentoring disaffected young people.

D1331830

About Diffusion books

Diffusion publishes books for adults who are emerging readers. There are two series:

 Books in the Diamond series are ideally suited to those who are relatively new to reading or who have not practised their reading skills for some time (approximately Entry Level 2 to 3 in adult literacy levels).

 Books in the Star series are for those who are ready for the next step. These books will help to build confidence and inspire readers to tackle longer books (approximately Entry Level 3 to Level 1 in adult literacy levels).

Other books available in the Diamond series are:

Space Ark by Rob Childs

Snake by Matt Dickinson

Fans by Niall Griffiths

Lost at Sea by Joel Smith

Uprising by Alex Wheatle

Other books available in the Star series are:

Not Such a Bargain by Toby Forward

Barcelona Away by Tom Palmer

Forty-six Quid and a Bag of Dirty Washing by Andy Croft

Bare Freedom by Andy Croft

One Shot by Lena Semaan

Nowhere to Run by Michael Crowley

This book has been produced in partnership with Reflex. Reflex exists to empower children, young people and young adults to break the cycle of offending and reoffending, equipping them with the skills, character and confidence to realize their full potential. www.reflex.org

Breaking the Chain

Darren Richards

diffusion

First published in Great Britain in 2017

Diffusion
an imprint of SPCK
36 Causton Street
London SW1P 4ST
www.spck.org.uk

ISBN 978-1-908713-08-7
eBook ISBN 978-1-908713-22-3

Typeset by Graphicraft Limited, Hong Kong
First printed in Great Britain by Ashford Colour Press
Subsequently digitally reprinted in Great Britain

Produced on paper from sustainable forests

For J. B.

*Thanks to my wife, for her support,
and to my boys who inspire me daily.
Also to Tim, Sam, Primi and Rebecca
for their wisdom and input.*

Contents

1
Eggs for breakfast

'Cell search! Stand by your doors,' shouted one of the officers.

Men stood by the doors of their cells. The dogs with the officers were given a bag to smell and a treat if they found something. It was a game for them.

Ken Atwater leaned on his walking stick and watched the sniffer dogs run about. He had seen them do this many times.

Ken was not someone you would pick out of a crowd. He was an old man with a narrow face and eyes that stood out like bright gems. He wore a tatty jumper which hung off his bony shoulders. The sleeves were bunched up like armbands.

The men called out and joked with their mates on the other side of the prison landing. It was a sound Ken was used to, like clanking doors and jingling keys.

Ken saw that one young man was losing his cool. A first-timer called Josh. Although Ken had not met him, he knew who Josh was. Josh had only arrived in the prison a few days ago but he was already causing trouble and getting a bad name.

'I shouldn't even be here!' yelled Josh. 'This is out of order!'

Josh was so angry he felt like screaming. His hands were shaking and he had knots in his belly. That morning, he had been given a letter from his girlfriend. It was the sort of letter every prisoner dreads. Josh had been with his girlfriend for a year and now she had broken up with him.

'Do you want a nicking?' an officer warned Josh. 'Settle down or you're going in the shower room until you calm down.'

Ken watched as Josh punched a wall and let out a yell.

'OK! That's enough!' the officer said crossly and he led Josh away.

'Poor kid,' thought Ken.

When the cell search was over, Ken saw Josh coming back on to the wing. He looked calm but fed up.

'Morning,' called out Ken. 'You look like you've had better days!'

Ken's voice sounded croaky. It was the first thing he had said that day.

'What?' asked Josh.

'I said, good morning. Do you know anyone yet?' asked Ken.

'No. Not yet,' said Josh.

'Well, I'm Ken. Most of the lads here call me Suds,' said Ken.

'I'm Josh. Why do they call you Suds?' asked Josh.

'It's a long story. Let's get some breakfast,' Ken said with a smile. 'I'll even give you my eggs. You had a rough start today.'

'Yeah, man. Thanks,' replied Josh.

What do you think?

- How would you describe Ken? What is he like? Do you like him?

- Why was Josh feeling angry? What else might Josh have been feeling?

- Think of a time when you lost your temper. How might things have been different if you had stayed calm? What are some good ways of controlling your anger and keeping calm?

2
Something happened

'The tea here is terrible,' said Ken, pulling a face.
'I prefer peppermint tea. But the breakfast isn't
too bad.'

'Thanks for this,' said Josh. He jabbed Ken's
fried eggs with a fork and flicked them on to
his plate. The yolks spilt, mixing with his baked
beans.

'So why are you called Suds?' asked Josh, with
a mouthful of eggs.

'Well, I never knew my real dad,' Ken said. 'But the man who adopted me told me I was found in a basket, on top of a washing machine.'

'You're joking,' said Josh.

'I am not,' said Ken, suddenly sounding serious. 'I was found on a washing machine next to the washing powder. That's why I'm called Suds.'

'So, you were adopted?' asked Josh.

'Sort of,' said Ken. He got up from the table to leave.

Free flow was starting. Soon prisoners would begin moving around the prison. Ken wanted to be back in his cell before the rush.

'That's it?' Josh asked, feeling a little short-changed.

'No, that's not *it*,' Ken answered. 'I haven't told you the best part yet.'

As they arrived back at Ken's pad, he said, 'Come in and I'll tell you the rest.'

Ken sat down on his bed and Josh sat on a chair by the table.

'I grew up in a big house, by a lake,' began Ken. 'The man who brought me up was very rich. He owned TV stations, newspapers, and that kind of thing. He was a powerful man. He even had the Prime Minister's private phone number.'

'Sweet deal!' Josh said with a grin.

'I was very lucky,' explained Ken. 'I had a great education. I had all my meals cooked by a chef. I even had a nanny! I had a lot of nice things and a lot of fun, but I would often wonder about my birth family.'

Ken sighed. He sat back on his bed and kicked off his shoes.

An officer came to the door of Ken's cell.

'Josh,' he said, 'I can take you to the gym now if you want to go.'

'No, thanks. I'm chatting to Suds,' replied Josh. He couldn't believe he was passing up a chance to work out, but he really wanted to hear the end of Ken's story.

The officer looked at Ken in surprise. Ken nodded, as if to say, 'It's fine, he's with me.'

'So, how did you end up in here?' asked Josh.

'There's a twist in this tale, lad. Something happened that changed everything,' said Ken with a smile.

What do you think?

- How does Ken feel about his childhood?

- Do you think that money can make a person happy? Why or why not?

- Can you think of a time when you got something you really wanted? How did it make you feel?

3
One-way ticket

'So,' said Josh, 'go on. Tell me how you ended up in prison.'

'OK,' said Ken. 'The twist is that my nanny turned out to be my mother. My real mother. I lived half my life not knowing who she was.'

Josh jumped to his feet in surprise and snapped his fingers. 'No way!' he said.

Ken took a deep breath and began to explain.

'One day my nanny came to find me,' said Ken. 'She was sobbing her heart out. By that time I was a grown man, but she still worked for my family. She told me that before I was born she had come to England from the Philippines with the couple who ended up adopting me. It turned out to be a one-way ticket.'

'Why "one way"?' Josh asked, looking surprised.

'She didn't know it at the time,' said Ken, 'but she was pregnant with me when she arrived in the UK. When she found out she was going to have a baby, she wanted to go back home to the Philippines. But my adoptive father wouldn't give her the money for the plane ticket. He told her that he and his wife would bring me up as their son. You see, they couldn't have any children of their own.'

'Why did she go along with that?' asked Josh.

'Because she was scared,' explained Ken. 'My adoptive father made it clear that she had no choice. She had no money and he took her passport away. He said that if she didn't go along with it, she would never see her child again. He said he would send my mother to work in another house, or he would smuggle her to another country.'

Then Ken said, 'I understand now that she was really like a slave in the house. As my nanny, at least she could raise me and keep me safe. She only agreed so she could stay with me.'

'You must have been so angry,' said Josh.

'Of course I was!' said Ken. 'All those years, she was trapped like a slave. I was out having a good time and my mum was suffering.'

Josh felt so sorry for Ken. He slumped back down on the chair.

'But, what hit me hardest was when I learned about my sister,' Ken explained. 'That's why my mother was crying and why she finally told me the truth. My mother told me I had an older sister, and that she was in trouble.'

Ken gripped the blanket until his knuckles turned white.

'What did you do?' asked Josh.

Ken looked straight at him with a cold stare. Josh felt the blood drain from his face.

'What did I do?' said Ken. 'I found my sister. That's why I got sent here.'

What do you think?

- Why didn't Ken's mum tell him her secret when Ken was younger?

- How do you think Ken felt about his adoptive parents, his nanny (his birth mother) and himself when he found out the truth?

- Can you think of a time when you have kept a secret from someone you care about? If you had told them your secret, how might things have been different?

4
Broken

The two men sat quietly for a moment, thinking about Ken's story.

Ken looked upset and Josh did not want to look him in the eyes. Instead Josh looked around the room. Ken kept his pad tidy. It almost felt like a home. Books and boxes were all stacked neatly. A thick blue cloth hung over the cell window, blocking out the light like a curtain.

'It's not bad in here,' Josh said.

'Thanks!' said Ken, laughing.

'OK. So, your nanny was your mum. Your dad was loaded, but he wasn't really your dad. And, you had a sister you never knew about?' asked Josh, thinking about everything Ken had told him.

'That's about it. You're smarter than you look,' joked Ken.

'That's messed up,' said Josh, shaking his head. 'So, then what happened?'

'I found out my sister had grown up in the Philippines,' explained Ken. 'When my mum came to England my sister was left with an aunt. My mum planned to earn some money and then go back to my sister. She wanted to give her a better life. My adoptive dad soon put an end to that. He would never let my mother leave.'

'That must have been so horrible for her,' said Josh.

'When my sister was older,' Ken said, 'she worked as a maid and a nanny. And, just like my mum, she came over to the UK with a family who promised her the earth. When she arrived, they took away her visa and passport.'

Then Ken said, 'Soon after my mum found out that my sister was living and working in a house just a few miles away. My mum's heart broke when she learned that her daughter had ended up like a slave, just like her.'

'Did she have it bad, like your mum?' asked Josh.

'Worse,' replied Ken. 'When I found her she was in a bad way. She didn't have enough to eat. And the family locked her in the house every day. Her arms were black and blue. They did terrible things to her.'

'She was really in trouble then?' asked Josh.

There were tears in Ken's eyes. He tipped his head back against the wall.

'She was. She was pregnant,' said Ken in a croaky voice.

Ken cleared his throat and then said, 'I told my sister she was coming with me. I told her I would look out for her. That's when the man who had hurt her and treated her like a slave showed up.'

'Did you kill him?' asked Josh, quickly.

'I felt a rage come over me. My mum had lived like a slave and now it was happening all over again to my sister. I lashed out,' said Ken.

'But he had it coming, didn't he?' said Josh.

'When I saw what I had done, I couldn't breathe,' Ken said. 'There was blood all over the floor. I thought I was going to pass out.

My heart was thumping, like it might burst out of my chest. I was sweating too, cold sweats. I've never known fear like it. It was the worst day of my life. That man had kids, and I took away their father.'

Josh did not know what to say.

Ken added, 'I didn't want my sister's baby to grow up thinking I was a hero. So I asked my sister to forget we ever met. Her child deserved a better start in life.'

'Then,' said Ken, 'I ran.'

What do you think?

- Why did Ken ask his sister to forget about him?

- Ken's birth mother and sister could be described as 'domestic slaves'. How do you think it would feel to live like that?

- Why did the man who treated Ken's sister so badly 'have it coming'? What other choices did Ken have?

- If you were Ken, what might you have done?

5

Breaking the chain

'I didn't know my old man, either,' said Josh
quietly.

'Is that right?' asked Ken.

'Yeah. It's always just been me and my mum,'
said Josh, shrugging.

Josh wore a new grey tracksuit and flashy
trainers. His hair was wavy, jet black and gelled
back. Above his top lip was a strip of fine hair.
He was too baby-faced for real stubble.

'If anyone ever hurt her,' Josh said, pointing his finger, 'I would put an end to them!'

Ken thought for a moment.

'If I had my time again, I would have walked away,' said Ken. 'And I would have taken my sister with me. I regret what I did.'

'But you saved her. Why regret it?' asked Josh. He was confused.

'Because you should always look after your family,' explained Ken. 'My mum gave up everything for me, and I just got banged up. While I was inside, there was nothing I could do to help my mum. I couldn't help my sister rebuild her life. I couldn't help with her baby. I failed them.'

'The man I killed was a nasty piece of work, but he had kids. Because of me they grew up without a father too. I wanted to make Mum proud. Instead, I just kept the pain going.'

'It wasn't your fault,' said Josh.

'Yes, it was,' replied Ken. 'I should have done better. My nephew didn't have a dad around, but he could have had me. And I let him down.'

Ken pointed to the door. 'This place is full of men who went through hell growing up. Son after son, without a dad. Every father in here wants better for his kids. One day you may have kids of your own, who will look up to you. Make sure you're smarter than I was. Break the chain,' he said.

'OK, man. I hear what you're saying,' said Josh. 'So, after you had killed the bloke, where did you go?'

'I slept rough,' Ken replied, taking a deep breath. 'You don't know cold, until you're on the streets. When you're tired, and wet to your bones. When folk just walk past and ignore you. You feel numb inside. Or you're spat at, kicked or worse.'

Josh shook his head sadly.

Ken said, 'I went from five-star restaurants to raiding bins, overnight. I remember a girl who shared her burger with me. It was the kindest thing. It was all she had, and she gave me half.'

'Then, you got nabbed?' said Josh.

'Yeah. One night I tried to break up a fight. I still thought I could tell people what to do,' Ken explained. 'But on the streets I was a nobody. They wouldn't listen to me. Then one guy said he knew who I was. He had seen my picture on TV. I got nicked not long after.'

'So that's why you're in prison now?' said Josh.

'Actually, it's not!' said Ken. Then he asked, 'How much do you know about bees?'

'About bees?' asked Josh, looking surprised. 'I don't know anything about bees.'

'I served my time, Josh, and I walked free,' Ken explained. 'In a way, bees are why I'm back in here again.'

'Yeah, right! Whatever you say!' He thought Ken had lost the plot. He turned to walk out.

'Hear me out, lad,' Ken called after him. 'You should hear this last part, believe me.'

What do you think?

- Why does Ken regret what he did?

- What does Ken mean by 'break the chain'?

- What makes a good dad or a good mum?

- What makes a good son or a good daughter?

6
The tattoo

'OK, so you're back in prison because of bees. Is that why you got your tattoo?' asked Josh, pointing at Ken's arm.

Ken had a tattoo around his forearm. It was a pattern made of bees, smoke and hexagons. In the middle were two words, 'Every Saint'.

'Yeah, I've always loved bees. They live in cells, for a start!' joked Ken, tapping the little hexagons on his arm. 'Honey is one of the best things you can eat, did you know that?'

Then Ken said, 'There are men in India who risk their lives hunting for honey. They climb to the top of trees that are forty metres high to find beehives. It's dangerous work. Some of the men are killed because they fall from the trees. Other men are bitten by deadly snakes. Some men are even attacked by tigers. They take those risks to feed their families.'

'Did you see that on TV or something?' asked Josh.

'I read about it,' Ken replied. 'I used to read a lot. It took me out of this cell, made the world bigger. I could lose myself in books.'

'What was it like, being stuck in here for all those years?' asked Josh.

'It was awful. I wasn't sure if I would make it,' Ken said. 'My mates forgot about me.

My so-called father disowned me. I was totally alone. To make things worse, my story was all over the papers back then. It was like having a bullseye painted on my back.'

'So, how did you get through it?' asked Josh.

'Well, I had a chip on my shoulder for a while,' Ken explained. 'I thought I was better than everyone else in here. I felt that because I had money and a posh education I shouldn't have been locked up with criminals. I wanted to get respect so I tried to throw my fists about. I wasn't a nice guy for a while. But I soon discovered there's always a bigger guy who can hit harder.'

'I can't imagine you being like that. What changed you?' asked Josh.

Ken looked Josh in the eye. 'Thinking about my sister's baby. That's what changed me.

In the end, that's what got me through,' said Ken in a hushed tone.

'Did your mum and sister keep in touch?' asked Josh.

'My mum couldn't,' said Ken. 'After I was arrested, my adoptive father sent her back to the Philippines. He was worried that the police would start asking questions. She was weak and unwell, worn down by everything that had happened to her. She died soon after. My sister wrote to me. I didn't want her to visit me in here, but her letters gave me strength. I started to write too.'

'What, like a diary?' asked Josh.

'No, I never did that,' said Ken. 'I wrote letters for some of the lads. I would help them write to their sweethearts, and their mothers!' He laughed.

'You get to know people when you write their letters,' Ken said. 'They all had such sad stories. I saw grown men cry. I learned that drink can rip families apart. And some guys were just trying to put food on the table, like the honey hunters in India. I shared their struggles and I became their voice. That's when I knew.'

'When you knew what?' asked Josh.

'That *these* were the people who understood me, and understood my story too. Other people had turned their back on me but inside I was accepted for who I was. These men had been knocked about by life. They had been hurt, just like my sister and my mum,' said Ken.

'You still haven't told me why you're *back* inside,' Josh said.

A smell from the kitchen drifted into Ken's cell. Roast chicken mixed with greasy chips.

'We had better go and eat,' said Ken. 'I'll tell you the rest over lunch. If you've got time?'

'You messing? Time is one thing I have got,' laughed Josh.

'All right then,' Ken replied. 'But I'll need to take you back a few years.'

What do you think?

- Why did Ken write letters in prison?

- Why did Ken feel that the other prisoners were 'his people'?

- When have you felt most supported?

- When have you supported others?

7
Every Saint

As Ken and Josh ate their lunch, Ken went on with his story.

It was five years ago, Ken said, and I was waiting outside the prison gate. It was a freezing cold day and I didn't even have a coat, but I felt good. I was free.

Probation had sorted me out with a lift to Every Saint Farm. It was a project that took in ex-offenders and ex-addicts. They were given a safe place that they could call home, and were taught new skills.

The car pulled up to take me to the farm, and I got in. I rubbed my hands by the heater. The driver didn't say much. After a while, he stopped at a service station. He made some excuse and asked me to hitchhike the rest of the way. It wasn't very far, he said.

I didn't want to make a scene, so I agreed. I went inside the service station.

It wasn't long before some truckers came in for dinner. They planned to sleep in their cabs, so I couldn't get a lift with them.

Later, a young woman walked in.

'Can anyone help me?' she begged. 'My car is overheating.'

Some of the truckers began wolf-whistling and saying rude things to her.

I didn't want to draw attention to myself. It was only my first night of freedom. But I couldn't stand by and do nothing. I could see how scared she was.

'OK, lads, leave it at that,' I was surprised to hear myself say.

One of the truckers stood up.

'Who asked you, mate?' he hissed, squaring up to me.

My mind flashed back to all the times I had used my fists to put others in their place. This had to be different.

'Look, one of us is going to have to get our hands cold and oily,' I said with a smile. 'It may as well be me. You stay and enjoy your grub.'

The truck driver gave me an angry look and then sat down to finish his supper.

I walked outside with the girl.

'Thanks for stepping in,' she said. 'I think you may have saved me there. By the way, I'm Bonnie.'

'No problem. I'm Ken. Now, where is this car?' I asked, feeling quite a hero.

I topped up the oil in the engine and the car started first time.

'You're not going anywhere near Dengie, are you?' I asked her.

'Every Saint Farm?' she asked.

'Yes! That's where I'm headed.' I was surprised she knew it.

'Hop in,' said Bonnie, opening the passenger door.

As we drove, Bonnie told me that she lived at the farm. Her dad was the owner.

'I have to ask,' Ken said. 'If I'm going to Every Saint Farm, you must know that I've just got out of prison. Why risk giving me a lift?'

We arrived at the farm. Bonnie turned off the engine.

'Because people change, that's why,' she said. 'You were a real gent, back there. Every saint has a past and every sinner has a future. Every Saint Farm, get it? Listen to me, I sound just like my dad!' Bonnie laughed.

My eyes filled with tears, which I quickly brushed away.

'Anyone you want to call? Let them know you're here safe?' asked Bonnie.

'Thanks, but no. I need a fresh start,' I explained.

There really was no one to contact. My mum had died while I was in prison. And my adoptive family and old friends wanted nothing to do with me. I planned to get in touch with my sister, but not until I was settled.

I got out of the car and took a deep breath, filling my lungs with cold, fresh air.

The farmhouse door was flung open and a large man walked towards us. A scruffy dog was running happily beside him.

'Hi, Dad,' said Bonnie, kissing her father on the forehead.

'Welcome, welcome. I'm Eddy. Come inside. We've got soup,' said Bonnie's dad. He wrapped his coat around me.

What do you think?

- How did Ken handle the truckers who taunted Bonnie and squared up to him?

- In what ways do you think Ken has changed?

- What could you change in the future by learning from your past?

8
Home

Ken told Josh more of his story as they ate together in the noisy wing.

I had never lived on a farm before, yet I felt as though I had come home.

I would spend hours outside, around the beehives with Eddy, learning about bees. He taught me how to make wild-flower honey, and how to fish. And we talked about the past. Eddy became like a second dad to me, but a dad I could trust.

I loved that farm. I lived there for five years. There were some golden moments. I loved being alone. I would listen to the birdsong and eat the fresh honey I collected. I can't remember a time when I had felt so calm and at peace. It was very different from being alone in a cell, surrounded by fighting and noise.

That's why I got this bee tattoo. I wanted other people to see me as a beekeeper, not an offender.

One sunny afternoon, I was by the hives watching the bees. Eddy came to find me. He looked serious.

'Ken,' said Eddy. 'I've just heard on the news. It's your father. He's passed away.'

I felt dizzy. The man I had called my father for so many years was gone.

'I don't know how to feel,' I said.

I knew I had to phone my sister. We had not spoken for a long time. Last I heard, she was doing well and working in an office. I had kept away because I didn't want her son to know that his uncle was a murderer. But at that moment I needed to talk to someone who would understand how I was feeling.

But as soon as she answered the phone, I could tell something was wrong. She sounded upset. It couldn't be because of my father's death. She hadn't even known him. It must be something else.

That was when she told me that my nephew was going to prison. He was being held in a jail near her house, but in a few weeks he would be transferred to another prison. The very same prison I had been released from.

My whole body went cold. I felt sick. I felt guilty. How could this happen?

As my sister explained more, I felt sure this boy was innocent.

That evening, Eddy found me with my head in my hands. He could tell I was upset.

'Let's go for a walk,' he said.

We walked down to the stream and along the bank. The sun was setting and the air was still.

'I've been so selfish. I've really let that boy down,' I told Eddy.

'Have you?' asked Eddy.

'I should have gone back to them, after I got out,' I explained. 'Then this would never have happened.'

'Don't blame yourself. Look at how far you've come,' said Eddy.

'But I walked away from them!' I said crossly.

When we got back to the house, Eddy put some crumpets on the stove.

'Eat this. You've got to eat,' said Eddy, with a kind smile.

It was good advice. The warm melted butter and sweet honey filled my mouth and lifted my spirits.

'Every saint has a bee in his halo,' said Eddy gently.

'What's that supposed to mean?' I asked.

'It means that good men live for something bigger than themselves. They live to help others. That's what I reckon, anyway!' Eddy laughed.

'What can I do?' I asked, feeling powerless.

'The kid is in prison. From everything my sister said, it sounds like he's been framed. But who is going to believe he's innocent if all he has is an ex-con like me to speak up for him?'

'You'll find a way to be heard,' Eddy replied, putting his hand on my shoulder. 'Think about what drives you. Your story, your skills, and your pain. You can use all that to help him. Think it over.'

Eddy left and I sat for hours, thinking and staring at the fire. Could I really give all this up? Could I walk away from Eddy and my new home? Should I throw it all away for a lad I had never even met?

As night turned to early morning, I made my decision. I got up and put the fire out. Then I wrote a note for Eddy and put it on the kitchen table. I tiptoed out of the door.

What do you think?

- How does Ken feel about Eddy and his life at Every Saint Farm?

- Why did he get a tattoo?

- What advice does Eddy give Ken? What do you think Ken will do next?

- What could you do to help change your family or community for the better?

9

There was a chance

By now Josh and Ken had finished eating their lunch. They cleared away their plates, and then walked back to Ken's cell.

Josh had listened carefully to Ken's life story. He had learned about the rich family that had adopted Ken. He understood why Ken had killed the man who was abusing his sister. He knew how Ken had struggled through a life sentence. It sounded as though Every Saint Farm was Ken's heaven on earth. Even his strange bee tattoo made sense now.

Josh believed what Ken had told him. As crazy as it all sounded, Ken's story had the ring of truth.

'So?' Josh said. 'Don't leave me hanging. What did you need to do? And why are you locked up again? Why throw that all away?'

Ken smiled. He drew in a long, slow breath, and let it out with a sigh. He chose his words carefully.

'Josh,' Ken said softly. 'It's you, lad.'

'What? What's me?' asked Josh, feeling confused.

'My sister's baby. It was you, Josh. You're my nephew,' explained Ken.

Ken's words landed like punches to Josh's gut. Josh stopped to catch his breath. His head was spinning.

'What are you talking about? You're crazy. That's not even funny!' Josh shouted. He was struggling to take it all in. 'You're nothing to do with me. I don't even have an uncle.'

'Wait, hear me out,' insisted Ken. 'When I left prison I agreed to certain rules. I agreed to live on the farm. And I agreed to stay away from the family of the man I killed. So I asked Eddy to tell the police that I had run away and that I was on my way to see the dead man's family. I breached my licence to serve out my sentence, so I could be here for you.'

'I never asked for this! I don't even know you!' said Josh, shaking his head. 'Why would you do that?'

'I couldn't visit you in prison, not with my record. And I couldn't write all I wanted to tell you in letters because that wouldn't be the same.

It had to be this way,' said Ken. His eyes were filled with tears.

'I don't need a babysitter, Ken, you weirdo!' shouted Josh.

An officer looked inside the cell. He told the men to settle down, then he moved away.

'Now, listen,' said Ken firmly. 'You've just got here. You don't know what prison is like. You don't know how tough it is in here. I want to be in here with you when things get hard. That's what family is about, remember.'

Josh slid down the cell wall and sank to the floor. His anger turned to sadness. He was holding back tears.

'Why the long story? Why not be straight with me?' Josh asked. His hands were shaking.

'There was a chance you wouldn't believe me,' Ken said softly. 'I needed you to hear the whole story. I needed you to trust me.'

Josh had nothing more to say. He looked at Ken sadly. Then he shook his head and walked out.

What do you think?

- Why did Ken come back to prison?

- How do you think Josh felt when he found out that Ken was his uncle?

- What do you think about Ken's decision to go back to prison? In what ways was it a good or bad decision?

- What could you do to help your family and friends when they go through tough times?

10
The beginning

The next morning, as soon as the cell doors were opened, Josh came to find Ken.

The two men talked for hours. Afterwards, Ken decided to write down the whole story. He was good at telling stories.

Ken wrote about his mother and his sister. He wrote about how they had been kept as slaves. He wrote about how Josh's mum struggled to provide for Josh. She had nowhere to go and no money to go back to the Philippines.

She took work wherever she could and moved from place to place.

Ken also wrote about why Josh should not be in prison. A masked gang had broken into a house and attacked an old couple. The gang members framed Josh. He had been in trouble with the police before and he didn't have friends and family to look out for him. He was an easy target.

Ken ended his story with a plea for justice. He asked for freedom for his nephew, and for people trapped in slavery. He was determined to do something to help.

Ken asked his sister to post his story online, with a petition linked to it. The petition called for more to be done to stop slavery. It also demanded support for women who had been trapped in slavery, like Josh's mum.

And it explained how children like Josh, whose mothers had been slaves, needed help too.

The online petition went viral. Women's rights groups and people-trafficking charities all supported Ken's call to action. Thousands of people painted the palms of their hands red, and uploaded photos of their hands on social media streams. This was a symbol that anyone who kept slaves had blood on their hands.

Over time, more and more people called for something to be done about domestic slavery. The petition was signed by over 150,000 people. The story was on the TV news, and Members of Parliament found themselves under real pressure to do something.

One MP made a speech demanding a retrial for Josh. 'We have to break this cycle,' he said. 'And we can start by helping Josh.'

Weeks turned into months. Ken was right there by Josh's side, to support him. He kept Josh out of trouble in prison, and helped him to work for some qualifications. Ken also helped to find somewhere safe for Josh to stay after he was released, away from old friends and bad influences.

Finally, Josh's case was heard at a retrial.

Josh's mum cried when she heard the jury's verdict. Josh was found 'not guilty'. He was cleared of all charges.

Crowds gathered outside the court. They cheered when they heard the news.

Ken was at the court. He had been called as a witness. After the verdict, he was allowed a moment to speak to Josh and his sister.

Josh gave Ken a huge smile. 'Well, Suds. I don't know what to say. How can I ever repay you?' he asked.

'Well, you could start by calling me Uncle!' joked Ken.

'Uncle Ken?' laughed Josh. 'Absolutely.'

As Josh got ready to leave, Ken handed him a book.

'It's about . . .' Ken began.

'Bees?' Josh guessed, with a smile.

'Ha! Bee*keeping*, actually. Honey never goes bad, lad. Make sure you don't either,' Ken said.

Ken reached out to shake Josh's hand, but Josh gave him a big hug.

'Thank you so much,' said Josh, quietly.

'Right, don't keep your fans waiting,' joked Ken. 'Be brave and stay strong.'

Josh turned and kissed his mum on the cheek. 'I need to do this,' he told her. 'I need a fresh start where I can be someone different. And maybe even help a few people. I'll make you proud, Mum.'

Outside the court, there was a sea of cameras and people with placards. Josh walked out and the crowd parted to let him through.

Ken saw a big man, with a dog by his side. It was Eddy.

'Good to meet you, Josh. You ready to go?' Eddy asked him.

'Yeah, I'm ready,' Josh replied.

Ken was led away and locked in a van. He could hear the crowd cheering outside.

Ken smiled as he pictured Josh meeting Bonnie at the farm. He wondered if he would get out in time to see Josh start a family of his own one day. Ken hoped so. He wanted to see for himself what a good father Josh was going to make.

What do you think?

- How would you describe the relationship between Ken and Josh by the end of the book?

- In what ways is Josh free? In what way is Ken free?

- What could you do to make someone proud of you?

Where to find out more

If you have been affected by the issues in this book, you could contact:

Modern Slavery Helpline
Telephone: 0800 012 1700

Salvation Army Adult Victims of Modern Slavery Helpline
Telephone: 0300 303 8151

Kalayaan (a charity that seeks justice for migrant domestic workers)
Telephone: 020 7243 2942
Address: St Francis of Assisi Community Centre, 13 Hippodrome Place, London W11 4SF
Email: info@kalayaan.org.uk
Website: www.kalayaan.org.uk